To Tyler,
Always enjoy the
magic of books!!
Lisa Funari Willever
2002

Maximilian
The
Great

Lisa Funari Willever
Lorraine Funari

Illustrated by Adam Corsi

Special Guest Young Author & Illustrator Section

Franklin Mason Press

To my daughter, Jessica Marie...LFW

To my husband, Rennie and my family. Thank you for believing in me...LF

To my wonderful parents, loving wife, and beautiful children, Melanie, Hannah, and Elijah...AC

★　★　★

The editors at Franklin Mason Press would like to offer their gratitude to those who have contributed their time and energy to this project: Mr. Donald Greenwood, Mr. Robert Quackenbush, Ms. Catherine Funari, Ms. Geraldine Willever, Sr. Marie Anthony, Mrs. Suzanne Rhoads, Mrs. Victoria Zupko-Demanovich, Mrs. Elizabeth H. Rossell, Mrs. Lisa Battinelli, Mr. Nick Candelori, Dr. Patricia Kempton, Ms. Wanda Bowman, Ms. Nancy Volpe, and Ms. Karen Aiello. Also, a special thanks to those who worked on the Guest Young Author and Guest Young Illustrator Committees. Your care in selecting the work of young authors and illustrators will help to shape and inspire the writers and illustrators of tomorrow.

Printed in Singapore

Franklin Mason Press ISBN No. 0-9679227-3-9

Library of Congress Control Number: 00-090880

Franklin Mason Press is proud to support the important work of the March of Dimes. In that spirit, $0.25 will be donated from the sale of each book. If you are pregnant or thinking of becoming pregnant and would like information on steps you can take to have a healthy baby, contact the March of Dimes at 888-MODIMES or www.MODIMES.org.

Pull up a chair and we'll have a nice chat,
about a magician and a used magic hat.

He once was a baker and Max was his name,
but the magic he tried never came out the same.

This hat had instructions, inside a black book,
but he thought he'd be fine and did not take a look.

Some tricks turned out messy. Some tricks turned out funny.
And I saw it all, because I was his bunny.

My name is Tahdah and I live in that hat,
with a frog and a dove and a little white cat.

He found us one day as he walked down the street,
when the wind blew our hat right up to his feet.

He picked up our hat. It was worn. It was dusty.
And the magic inside may have been a bit rusty.

But Max was determined, he worked day and night.
He tried every trick, but none came out right!

With a wave of his wand and just one mixed up spell,
the dove was a pickle, the frog was a bell!

And the cat, the poor cat, had the very worst luck,
for Max turned him into ... a red fire truck!

He made up new tricks and he practiced each spell,
but still Max's magic did not work out well.

Now, the very next day, was his very first show
and Maximilian The Great was determined to go.

He arrived at the school at a quarter past nine
and he hoped and he prayed, that things would go fine.

He stood on the stage with his cape and his wand
and the principal whispered, "Maximilian, you're on!"

"For my very first trick, I will pull out a dove."
But out of that hat ... came a polka dot glove!

"Next," Max declared, "I will pull out a puppy."
But a fishbowl appeared, with one tiny guppy!

He was scared. He was nervous. He just could not think.
He reached for a sandwich, but pulled out a drink!

His hands started shaking and much to his dread,
he thought of the book that he wished he had read.

But instead of the book, ol' Max grabbed my ear,
then he hollered, "Tahdah," and they started to cheer!

So he took a big bow as the clapping grew louder.
Maximilian The Great, could not have been prouder.

And just when he thought he was on the right path,
the cat ran away ... when he sawed her in half!

And the frog and the dove, they disrupted the act,
when the frog gave the dove ... a ride on his back!

But they loved each mistake, much to Max's surprise.
And their clapping, it brought, happy tears to his eyes!

So maybe his magic was not up to par,
but the kids sure had fun and that's better by far.

Later that evening, Max found the black book
and he thought, maybe now, he would take a quick look.

In search of the secrets he knew he would need,
he opened the book and he started to read:

"To be a magician,
to do magic well,
you don't need a wand
you don't need a spell."

"You need a good heart
to be good at this craft.

Real magic...is really
to make others laugh!"

The End

Kathleen Morrison
Age 9 — Littlebrook School
Princeton, New Jersey

That's My Dragon!

"Wow!" said Emily. The speckled, leathery egg in her hand wobbled. It wiggled, the shell cracked, and out came a small lizard. "I wonder what Mrs. Finchspokel will say about this," Emily wondered. She tucked the little animal into her backpack and started running down the street so she wouldn't be late for school. Suddenly, Emily's backpack started to expand. With a loud, "POP!", it burst. Books and papers flew everywhere. As she gathered them up, she noticed that the once small lizard had become a 2,000 pound dragon. It was even bigger than a van! "Wow!" yelled Emily. The dragon had sharp horns and scaly skin. It had a long, strong tail. If it wanted to, the dragon could sweep down small trees. It had a long neck that stretched toward the heavens. The huge dragon looked down at Emily. "Do you want a ride?" the dragon asked. Emily's eyes sparkled. "Sure!" Emily climbed up on the dragon. "What is your name?" she asked, after she was safely on top. "Norbert," said the dragon. "My name is Emily." When the two friends got to school, Norbert said, "This is where I leave you." "Goodbye," said Emily as the dragon flew off into the distance.

A few years later... "In the jungles of China, a huge lizard has been spotted," the TV blared. Emily smiled to herself, "That's my dragon!"

Emily Petersack
Age 9 — Mercerville School
Hamilton, New Jersey

"The Lottery Ticket"

Jeffery Hugh Cooper
Age 9 — Mercerville School
Hamilton, New Jersey

"On The Way To School"

Guest Young Illustrator

Daniel Piotrowski
Age 8 — Langtree School
Hamilton, New Jersey
"Fishing With Pop Pop"

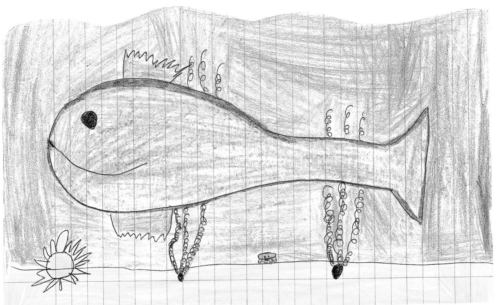

Christine Richin
Age 7 — Roosevelt School
River Edge, New Jersey

Julia Kim
Age 8 — Perry L. Drew School
East Windsor, New Jersey

Would You Like To Be An Author or Illustrator?

Franklin Mason Press is looking for stories and illustrations from children ages 6-9 to appear in our books. We are dedicated to providing young authors and illustrators with an avenue into the world of publishing.

If you would like to be our next Guest Young Author or Guest Young Illustrator, read the information below and the rules on the next page.

To be a Guest Young Author :

Write a 100-200 word story about something your family does that is funny.

To be a Guest Young Illustrator :

Draw a picture of your favorite place.

Prizes

1st. Place Author / 1st. Place Illustrator
$25.00 and your work will be published in FMP's newest book.

2nd. Place Author / 2nd. Place Illustrator
$15.00 and your name will be published in FMP's newest book.

3rd. Place Author / 3rd. Place Illustrator
$10.00 and your name will be published in FMP's newest book.

Tips

1. Let others read your work. Ask them to check for mistakes and to give you their opinion. Keep rewriting until your work is perfect.
2. Write about things you enjoy and things that you know about.
3. Find a nice, quiet place to write or draw.
4. Remember, the best writers and illustrators are people who enjoy reading books!

Rules For The Contest

1. Children may enter one category only, either Author or Illustrator.
2. All stories must be typed.
3. All illustrations must be sent in between two pieces of cardboard to prevent wrinkling.
4. Name, address, phone number, age, school, and parent's signature must be on the back of all submissions.
5. All work must be original and completed solely by the child.
6. Franklin Mason Press reserves the right to print submitted material. All work becomes property of FMP and will not be returned. Any work selected is considered a work for hire and FMP will retain all rights.
7. There is no deadline for submissions. FMP will publish children's work in every book published. All submissions will be considered for the next available book.
8. All submissions should be sent to:Youth Submissions Editor, Franklin Mason Press, P.O. Box 3808, Trenton, NJ 08629
www.franklinmason.com

About The Authors And Illustrator

Lisa Funari Willever (author) is a lifelong resident of Trenton, New Jersey and a fourth grade teacher in the Trenton School District. She is a graduate of The College of New Jersey and a member of the New Jersey Education Association and the New Jersey Reading Association. The author of *The Culprit Was A Fly, Miracle On Theodore's Street,* and *Everybody Moos At Cows,* this is her fourth children's picture book. Her husband, Todd, is a professional Firefighter in the city of Trenton and the co-author of *Miracle On Theodore's Street.* They are the proud parents of one year old, Jessica Marie.

Lorraine Funari (author) is a lifelong resident of Mercer County, New Jersey and the mother of three grown children, Lisa, Anthony, and Paula. Her husband, Reynold, is a meat cutter in Ewing, New Jersey. She has co-authored several upcoming children's books with her daughter, Lisa.

Adam Corsi (illustrator) is a native of Philadelphia, Pennsylvania and currently lives in Upper Darby, PA with his wife, Jennifer, and their three children, Melanie, Hannah, and Elijah. Adam has illustrated three children's books, *The Culprit Was A Fly, Miracle On Theodore's Street,* and *Everybody Moos At Cows.* In addition to illustrating, Adam is a commercial designer with Renald M. Corsi & Associates.

Franklin Mason Press

P.O. Box 3808, Trenton, NJ 08629
www.franklinmason.com